FROM THE ILLUSTRATOR: Dedicated to Mike Shealy whose heart was as big as the whole outdoors. His love of the Earth and all her creatures was contagious. I would not have been able to tackle a mountain in search of a little lost llama without him.

FROM THE AUTHOR: To Everett and Jack, who were my first audience, and whose enthusiasm for Homer's story, and all our stories, propels me ever forward.

www.mascotbooks.com

The Little Lost Llama

For more information, please contact:
Mascot Books
620 Herndon Parkway, Suite 320
Herndon, VA 20170
info@mascotbooks.com

Library of Congress Control Number: 2018904778

CPSIA Code: PRT0718A
ISBN-13: 978-1-68401-987-8

Printed in the United States

Written by
MARIE BALLARD

Illustrated by
TRACY DUCHARME

T. DUCHARME

The Little Lost Llama

A happy little llama ran and played with his llama friends among the tall grasses and sweet smelling wildflowers on his Colorado ranch. He lived at the bottom of a big, snowcapped mountain called Pikes Peak.

One night while the little llama was snuggled up to his mama, dreaming sweet dreams, a hungry mountain lion attacked. The little llama was frightened. He didn't want to leave his mother, but he knew he had to go. He ran.

He ran and ran, faster and farther than he had ever run before. He ran up and up, away from his home, past groves of aspen, scrub oak, and pine. Finally, exhausted, he came to a little mountain town.

The little llama sensed he wasn't alone. He saw eyes glowing up ahead. What was it? Dogs!

The pack of dogs growled and snarled, snapping at his feet. The little llama turned and ran again, faster and faster, out of town and up the mountain side, leaving the snarly dogs far behind.

The next day as a brilliant golden sun rose in a brilliant blue sky, the little llama realized he was lost. Some new and interesting animals watched nervously. There was a marmot, a ground squirrel, a fox, and a skunk. Cautiously, he approached them.

The mountain animals were worried. They had never seen a llama on their mountain before. They sensed danger. With a loud whistle, the marmot signaled the other animals, and they scampered away.

The little llama trotted on up the mountain and came upon some bighorn sheep munching on the alpine grass. Would they help a little lost llama? Cautiously, he approached them.

But bighorn sheep are shy and not used to strangers. They were startled by the new suspicious animal. Quickly, they climbed higher into the safety of the steep rocks. The llama tried to follow, but they were too fast and nimble and disappeared among the craggy boulders.

Suddenly the little llama heard chuga, chuga, chuga, chuga, choo, choo. A train was slowly winding its way up the mountain. People were staring out the window, pointing and snapping photos. The llama was surprised to see humans on this mountain. The humans were surprised to see a llama, but the train didn't stop or even slow down.

The little llama was hungry and cold as the sun sank behind the mountain peaks. The night grew colder and colder. He missed his llama family and the ranch.

Tomorrow he would try again to make friends with those shy bighorn sheep and maybe even that pesky marmot. He found a quiet protected space beneath the stars, and humming to himself softly, he fell asleep.

Meanwhile, the story of the little lost llama was on TV and in the newspapers. The people in the city worried he might be in danger. The winter storms were coming, and there were mountain lions, bears, and coyotes on the prowl. How could they help him? Why was he on the mountain? Where were his owners?

The little lost llama heard the familiar chuga, chuga of the cog train. He had been lost on the mountain for six weeks now, and he liked watching and chasing after the train. Then one day some humans ran up to him by the tracks and tried to lasso him. He was frightened. He signaled his distress with a loud hum, but the rangers kept trying to rope him. The llama was scared so he ran, escaping higher into the mountain.

The wind howled all through the cold night. An early winter storm dumped several feet of snow on the mountain. The little lost llama had tucked himself away in an overhanging rocky area, out of the worst of the blizzard.

Looking for one little white llama in a blizzard is almost impossible, but two llama ranchers, Tracy and Mike, were once again on Pikes Peak searching for him. They had searched before unsuccessfully. They drove up to the top of the mountain and started hiking down. They had brought their own llamas with them, hoping the lost llama would not be afraid.

Suddenly, Tracy spotted the little lost llama! He was below her on the mountain. He looked healthy though a little thin. Tracy knew this would be her best chance to rescue him, but the little lost llama was so busy playing with the marmot and ground squirrels, he didn't notice her.

"Come on, Dancer," she said. "Let's go get this little llama."

Later that morning, when the storm quieted, the little lost llama ventured out of his protected space. He saw a most surprising and welcoming sight. Another llama was cautiously approaching him, making his way slowly over the rough, frozen ground.

The other llama looked friendly, but the little lost llama noticed that he was with a woman. The little llama thought about running away again. Then he thought about how cold and hard it was to live on the mountain, all alone away from his family who he missed very much. Heart pounding, he ran to them.

"Hello little llama," Tracy said softly. "We've been looking all over for you. Let's go home." She gently placed a rope around his neck. "I will call you Homer, because of your great adventure."

Homer followed his new friends to their trailer and climbed in after Dancer. As they started down the mountain, Homer snuggled up to Dancer and went fast asleep. Word quickly spread among the mountain rangers, the cog train employees, tourists, journalists, and ranchers. The little lost llama had been rescued!

And just like that, the little lost llama wasn't lost or lonely anymore. Today, Homer lives at the bottom of that same big mountain called Pikes Peak with his rescuer, Tracy, two big rambunctious black dogs, his old friend Dancer, and his adopted llama family. He has found his home at last!

EPILOGUE

In September of 2009, travelers on the Pikes Peak Cog Train noticed a baby llama high on Pikes Peak near Manitou Springs, Colorado. Indigenous to the Andes Mountains of South America, llamas are domesticated and not kept on Pikes Peak. The little llama would frequently approach the train, but then run away. He evaded capture by well-meaning park rangers and the cog train employees. He was seen trailing after the bighorn sheep who wanted nothing to do with him. His confrontation with the dogs in Divide, Colorado, was also documented.

Worried about the vulnerable young llama with winter approaching, llama ranchers from the area had been searching Pikes Peak for weeks. Tracy duCharme and Mike Shealy, two of the local llama ranchers, set out again amidst an early winter storm. They brought llamas with them, hoping llamas' intense herding instinct would entice the baby llama to come to them.

Tracy and Mike separated on the mountain, and Tracy, with her adult llama, Dancer, saw the little white llama first. He didn't notice her at first because, despite the winter storm, he was playing among some other mountain animals.

He was indeed overjoyed to be found, and allowed Tracy to slip a lead rope around his neck and then a halter. He nuzzled up to his new llama friend. He followed Tracy and Dancer happily to her trailer at the top of Pikes Peak. Tracy named the llama Homer because of his amazing odyssey on the mountain where he had survived for six weeks. He was thin and suffered frostbitten ears, but was otherwise healthy and unharmed from his adventure. Tracy kept the llama at her ranch and continued her search for Homer's owner.

A mountain lion had killed the mother llama, and the owner assumed the baby llama had met the same fate. The owner left town shortly thereafter and did not see the local and national stories circulating about the lost llama on Pikes Peak. Finally, the media buzz caught up with her, and she contacted Tracy.

Today, Homer is living the good life on his ranch in Colorado with his rescuer and the illustrator of this book, Tracy duCharme, while Pikes Peak, the site of his odyssey, looms majestically on the horizon.

ANIMALS ON PIKES PEAK

Homer tried to befriend some of the animals on Pikes Peak: the yellow-bellied marmot, bighorn sheep, and ground squirrels. Black bears, elk, foxes, mountain lions, deer, raccoons, skunks, and chipmunks also call Pikes Peak home.

Marmots are the most populous of the animals on the mountain. They like to sun themselves on

the rocks during the summer and hibernate during the winter. Though generally friendly, the marmot will give a sharp whistle when it senses danger. Guess what its nickname is— the whistle-pig!

Pikes Peak also has a large population of bighorn sheep, Colorado's state animal. They are very shy and famous for their ability to climb almost vertical cliffs. Both of these characteristics made it difficult for Homer to befriend the bighorn sheep though he tried and tried. They are herbivores; Homer didn't need to worry about them eating him for lunch. This is not the case with mountain lions, which are carnivores and will attack a small mammal.

Homer's natural instinct told him to climb higher and higher to avoid predators. He was right! The animals and plants change and become more sparse higher up on the mountain. Why do you think that happens?

DO LLAMAS REALLY SPIT?

AND OTHER LLAMA FACTS

Llamas (scientific name: llama gama) originated in South America and are domesticated, rather than animals of the wild. They are relatives of the camel but without the hump. Like the camel, they can survive with very little water, and they are herbivores who will eat almost any kind of plants. They are sturdy and sure footed.

Native people of the Andes Mountains in South America have used llamas for thousands of years as pack and farm animals. Their wool is harvested for rope, yarn, and fabric. Many llamas have been imported to the United States as pets or as working animals on farms.

And what about that spitting? Well, yes, they do spit, if mistreated or in severe distress, but usually they spit at other llamas and not at humans. Llamas are friendly, respectful, and smart. They hum as a way of comforting themselves. They are very sociable, and they like being around others. Homer was lonely during the six weeks he was lost on the mountain because the other animals weren't quite ready to make friends with him. It is also why his rescuers took their own llamas with them to soothe him and encourage the lost llama to come to them.

Have a book idea?

Contact us at:

info@mascotbooks.com | www.mascotbooks.com